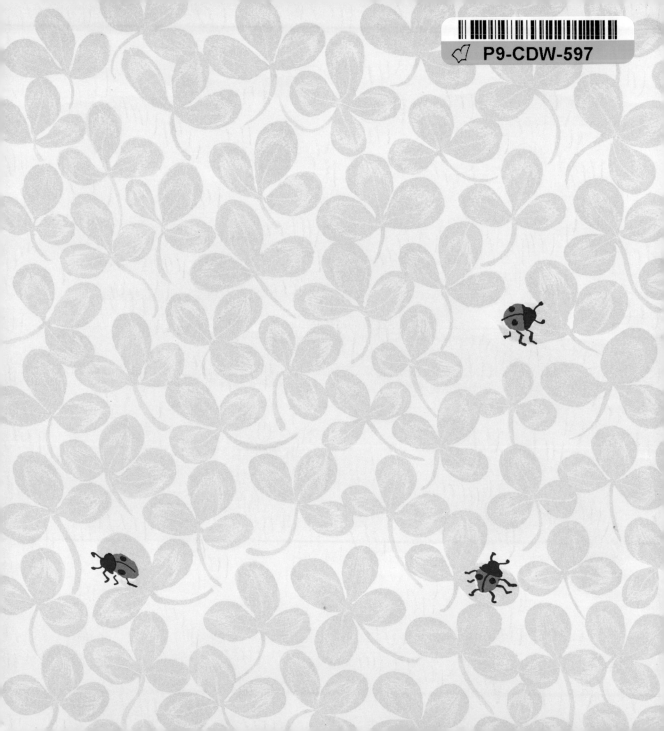

To Mart and Jean, who build houses too.

Clarion Books
a Houghton Mifflin Company imprint
215 Park Avenue South, New York, NY 10003
Copyright © 1970 by Paul Galdone
Copyright © renewed 1998 by Paul F. Galdone and Joanna C. Galdone

Printed in the USA.

Catalog Card Number: 75-123456.
Book designed by Paul Galdone.

RNF ISBN 0-395-28813-4
PAP ISBN 0-89919-275-0

WOZ 50 49 48 47 46 45 44

(Previously published by The Seabury Press
under ISBN 0-8164-3071-3)

The THREE LITTLE PIGS

PAUL GALDONE

Once upon a time
there was an old sow with three little pigs.
She had no money to keep them,
so she sent them off to seek their fortune.

The first little pig met a man
with a bundle of straw,
and said to him:
"Please, man, give me that straw
to build me a house."

So the man did,
and the little pig
built his house with it.

Along came a wolf.

He knocked at the door, and said:

"Little pig, little pig, let me come in."

"No, no," said the little pig.

"Not by the hair of my chinny chin chin."

"Then I'll huff, and I'll puff,

and I'll blow your house in," said the wolf.

So the wolf huffed, and he puffed,
and he blew the house in.
And he ate up the first little pig.

The second little pig
met a man
with a bundle
of sticks,
and said:
"Please, man,
give me those sticks
to build me a house."

So the man did,
and the little pig built his house with them.

Then along came the wolf, and said:
"Little pig, little pig,
let me come in."

"No, no! Not by the hair
of my chinny chin chin."

"Then I'll huff, and I'll puff,
and I'll blow your house in,"
said the wolf.

So he huffed, and he puffed,
and he huffed and he puffed, and
at last he blew the house in.
And he ate up the second little pig.

The third little pig
met a man
with a load of bricks,
and said:
"Please, man,
give me those bricks
to build me a house."

So the man did,
and the little pig built his house with them.

Soon the same wolf came along,
and said:
"Little pig, little pig,
let me come in."

"No, no! Not by the hair
of my chinny chin chin."

"Then I'll huff, and I'll puff,
and I'll blow your house in,"
said the wolf.

Well, he huffed, and he puffed
and he huffed and he puffed
and he huffed and he puffed.

But he could *not* blow the house in.

At last the wolf stopped
huffing and puffing, and said:
"Little pig, I know where there is
a nice field of turnips."

"Where?" said the little pig.

"On Mr. Smith's farm," said the wolf.
"I will come for you tomorrow morning.
We will go together,
and get some turnips for dinner."

"Very well," said the little pig.
"What time will you come?"

"Oh, at six o'clock," said the wolf.

Well, the little pig got up at five.
He went to Mr. Smith's farm,
and got the turnips
before the wolf came to his house.

"Little pig, are you ready?" asked the wolf.

The little pig said, "Ready!

I have been and come back again

and I got a nice potful of turnips for my dinner."

The wolf was very angry.
But then he thought of another way
to get the little pig, so he said:
"Little pig, I know where
there is a nice apple tree."

"Where?" said the pig.

"Down at Merry Garden," replied the wolf.
"I will come for you
at five o'clock tomorrow morning
and we will get some apples."

Well, the little pig got up
the next morning at four o'clock,
and went off for the apples.
He wanted to get back home before the wolf came.
But it was a long way to Merry Garden,
and then he had to climb the tree.
Just as he was climbing back down
with his basket full of apples,
he saw the wolf coming!

"Little pig!" the wolf said.
"You got here before me!
Are the apples nice?"

"Yes, very," said the little pig.
"I will throw one down to you."
And he threw the apple as far as he could throw.
While the wolf ran to pick it up,
the little pig jumped down and ran home.

The next day the wolf came again
and said to the little pig: "Little pig, there is a fair
at Shanklin this afternoon. Would you like to go?"

"Oh, yes," said the little pig.
"When will you come to get me?"

"At three," said the wolf.

Well, the little pig went off at two o'clock
and bought a butter churn at the fair.

He was going home with it
when he saw the wolf coming!

The little pig jumped into the butter churn to hide.

The churn fell over and rolled
down the hill with the little pig in it.
This frightened the wolf so much
that he turned around and ran home.

Later the wolf went to the little pig's house
and told him what had happened.
"A great round thing came rolling down the hill
right at me," the wolf said.

"Hah, I frightened you then," said the little pig.
"I went to the fair and bought a butter churn.
When I saw you, I got into it,
and rolled down the hill."

The wolf was very angry indeed.
"I'm going to climb down your chimney
and eat you up!" he said.

When the little pig heard the wolf on the roof—

he hung a pot
full of water in the fireplace.
Then he built a blazing fire.
Just as the wolf was coming down the chimney,
the little pig took the cover off the pot,
and in fell the wolf.
The little pig quickly put on the cover again,
boiled up the wolf, and ate him for supper.

And the little pig lived happily ever afterward.